LITTLE SIMON

An imprint of Simon & Schuster Children's Publishing Division

1230 Avenue of the Americas, New York, New York 10020

First Little Simon hardcover edition January 2021

Text copyright © 2016 by Katharine Holabird

Illustrations copyright © 2016 by Sarah Warburton

Originally published as *Twinkle Tames a Dragon* in Great Britain in 2016 by Hodder Children's Books

LITTLE SIMON is a registered trademark of Simon & Schuster, Inc.,

and associated colophon is a trademark of Simon & Schuster, Inc.

For information about special discounts for bulk purchases, please contact

Simon & Schuster Special Sales at 1-856-506-1949 for business@simonandschuster.com.

Manufactured in China 1020 SCP

2 4 6 8 10 9 7 5 3 1

Cataloging-in-Publication Data is available from the Library of Congress.

ISBN 978-1-5344-2919-2

ISBN 978-1-5344-2920-8 (eBook)

# Twinkle's Fairy Pet Day

*Katharine Holabird and Sarah Warburton*

LITTLE SIMON

New York  London  Sydney  Toronto  New Delhi

Twinkle wanted a pet more than anything,
and so did her best friends Pippa and Lulu.
Twinkle even made up a special song:

# Twinkle's Fairy Pet Day

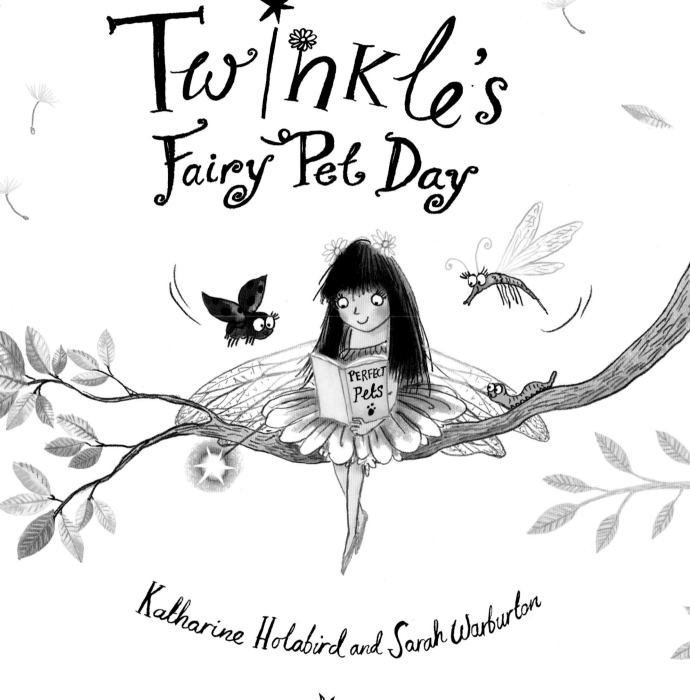

*Katharine Holabird and Sarah Warburton*

**LITTLE SIMON**
New York  London  Sydney  Toronto  New Delhi

Twinkle wanted a pet more than anything,
and so did her best friends Pippa and Lulu.
Twinkle even made up a special song:

"I've waited and wished
for such a long time...
for a sweet little pet who
will truly be mine!"

When Fairy Godmother heard Twinkle's song, she invited all three
fairies to the palace. "You're now old enough to take care of a pet," she said,
"so let's make your wishes come true. Pippa, what's your pet spell?"

"Abracadabra,
skiddledee~pie,
my pet loves to
swoop and fly!"

Pippa waved her wand gracefully, and in a sparkly flash
a gorgeous butterfly appeared.

"Fairytastic!
I LOVE butterflies!"
said Pippa.

Then it was Lulu's turn.

"*Abracadabra, skiddledee-pop,
my pet loves to jump and hop!*"

A glittery ladybug
landed on Lulu's head.
"Ooooh, lovely!"
said Lulu.

Twinkle couldn't wait for her sweet little pet to arrive. She swooshed her wand wildly around her head and then she said her spell:

"Abracadabra, skiddledee~day, my pet loves to run and play!"

The walls shook, the chandelier swayed, purple smoke poured
out of the fireplace, and then out popped . . .

. . . a little dragon!

"Fiddlesticks and fairycakes!"
exclaimed Twinkle.
"I really wanted something cute and fluffy,
**not** a dragon!"

"He just needs a little bit of training, that's all," said Fairy Godmother, avoiding the puffs of smoke. "Now, why don't you all bring your pets to Fairy Pet Day? There'll be prizes and fun for everyone!"

But Scruffy needed more than just a bit of training . . .

He gobbled up Twinkle's fairy cakes, left muddy footprints everywhere, and even chewed her best slippers!

Twinkle decided it was time for . . .

# . . . dragon training!

"Please fetch the ball now, Scruffy," said Twinkle, as Scruffy happily galloped past her.

"Okay, try jumping this fence," said Twinkle, but the little dragon was snoring under a tree.

"Please be a good little dragon and sit now, Scruffy," said Twinkle. But Scruffy just wagged his tail and ran around in circles.

"Oh dear," said Twinkle, tickling Scruffy's tummy, "I'll never be able to train you in time!"

When Fairy Pet Day at the Palace arrived,
Twinkle scrubbed and brushed Scruffy until his scales
were shining. She tied a pretty ribbon in his topknot,
and gave him a fancy new collar.

"You'll surely win a prize for being cute even if you are the naughtiest dragon in the forest," Twinkle said.

But on the way to the palace, Scruffy jumped in a great big puddle and splashed mud everywhere!

"Oh no!" sighed Twinkle.
"We'll never win anything now."

# Fairy Pet Day

The palace was crowded with fairies and their pets.
Everyone applauded as Pippa's butterfly won a prize for prettiest
pet, and Lulu's ladybug won a prize for her clever tricks.

It was soon time for the best-trained pet award. Twinkle knew Scruffy didn't have a chance, but she loved her new pet anyway.

"Just do your best, Scruffy," she whispered.

Scruffy cocked his ears and gazed sweetly at Twinkle as she tossed a ball high into the sky.

"Go, Scruffy!" Twinkle shouted. Scruffy **zoomed** off like a rocket,

did a few loop-the-loops,

and disappeared . . .

But then the little dragon raced back through the clouds
and dropped the ball at Twinkle's feet.

"Hooray!" everyone cheered.

"Congratulations," said Fairy Godmother
as she gave Twinkle and Scruffy their prize.
"What a well-trained little dragon."

Twinkle was so proud, her wings glowed rainbow colors,
and she sang happily to Scruffy:

"Scruffy is my dragon
and he loves to run and play...
He's the best pal ever, and
I love him more each day!"

BEST
TRAINED
PET

Tweeker

Bumpy

Bristle

Nutter

Snuffles

Flitter

Hopper